Dear Parent:

Congratulations! Your child is taking
the first steps on an exciting journey.
The destination? Independent reading!

STEP INTO READING® will help your child get there. The program offers
five steps to reading success. Each step includes fun stories and colorful art.
There are also Step into Reading Sticker Books, Step into Reading Math
Readers, Step into Reading Write-In Readers, Step into Reading Phonics
Readers, and Step into Reading Phonics First Steps! Boxed Sets—a complete
literacy program with something for every child.

Learning to Read, Step by Step!

Ready to Read Preschool–Kindergarten
• big type and easy words • rhyme and rhythm • picture clues
For children who know the alphabet and are eager to
begin reading.

Reading with Help Preschool–Grade 1
• basic vocabulary • short sentences • simple stories
For children who recognize familiar words and sound out
new words with help.

Reading on Your Own Grades 1–3
• engaging characters • easy-to-follow plots • popular topics
For children who are ready to read on their own.

Reading Paragraphs Grades 2–3
• challenging vocabulary • short paragraphs • exciting stories
For newly independent readers who read simple sentences
with confidence.

Ready for Chapters Grades 2–4
• chapters • longer paragraphs • full-color art
For children who want to take the plunge into chapter books
but still like colorful pictures.

STEP INTO READING® is designed to give every child a successful
reading experience. The grade levels are only guides. Children can progress
through the steps at their own speed, developing confidence in their
reading, no matter what their grade.

Remember, a lifetime love of reading starts with a single step!

www.stepintoreading.com

Educators and librarians, for a variety of teaching tools, visit us at
www.randomhouse.com/teachers

Library of Congress Cataloging-in-Publication Data
Scarry, Richard. Richard Scarry's watch your step, Mr. Rabbit! / by Richard Scarry.
    p.   cm. — (Step into reading. A step 1 book)
SUMMARY: Mr. Rabbit's feet get stuck in the street as he looks at his newspaper.
ISBN 0-679-88650-8 (trade) — ISBN 0-679-98650-2 (lib. bdg.)
[1. Rabbits—Fiction.] I. Title: Watch your step, Mr. Rabbit!   II. Title.   III. Series: Step
into reading. Step 1 book. PZ7.S327 Wat   2003   [E]—dc21   2002013767

Printed in the United States of America 25 24 23 22 21

STEP INTO READING, RANDOM HOUSE, and the Random House colophon are registered trademarks
of Random House, Inc.

Richard Scarry's
Watch Your Step, Mr. Rabbit!

Random House 🏠 New York

Here comes Mr. Rabbit.

Is he looking

at his feet?

6

No.

He is looking
at his newspaper.

Now he is looking
at his feet.
His feet are stuck
in the street.

Can we push him out?

No!

Can we pull him out?

No!

Can we blow him out?

16

No!

Can we squirt him out?

No, we cannot!

His feet are
good and stuck.

Aha!

We can scoop him out!

24

Mr. Rabbit

is not stuck now.

There goes Mr. Rabbit.

He is looking

at his newspaper again.

Oh, no!

Watch your step, Mr. Rabbit!